Things Left Unsaid

Elexis Bell

3

ELEXIS BELL

THINGS LEFT UNSAID

Eager to stay up to date on the latest dark literary fiction from Elexis Bell?

Sign up for her newsletter (and get a free short story) at:

www.elexisbell.com

To all the people out there putting up with red flags for the sake of giving someone another chance…

Draw a line.

If they cross it, leave.

Whether you believe it or not, you deserve better.

Prologue
Kurt

The car bumps along on the old dirt road as Ian hits yet another pothole. Elbows dig into both my sides as Jake and Kerry ricochet in their seats. I hold myself rigid, digging my feet into the floorboard to brace myself.

You'd think they'd try a little harder to keep from jabbing me. It isn't that hard to keep control of your parts.

Staring forward at Ian and Ariella in the front seats, I seethe, wishing I could sit there. But my hips are narrower than Ariella's, making me a better fit for this stupid seat. And it's Ian's stupid, tiny car, so of course, he's driving.

And she called it, so *eager* as she shouted, "Shotgun!"

My eyes roll as I stare out at the trees choking the road. Yet again, I question the point of this trip.

Her words from yesterday echo in my mind. "Come on, Kurt. You know I love haunted places. And I haven't seen Ian or Jake or Tori in so long."

Now, she sits in front, bathed in sunlight and beaming at Ian. They laugh together, recalling old college memories. Their arms bump together on the armrest with each dip in the road.

Ariella tips her head back, laughing deeply. She covers her mouth with her hand, but when she puts her arm back on the armrest, it lands skin to skin with Ian's.

And she barely pulls away.

Heat surges through my veins as anger burns me. I grit my teeth.

Ian swerves, hitting another pothole. Laughter fills the front seat as their arms brush again. Elbows dig into my sides. Again.

Fucking bastard's doing it on purpose…

And suddenly, I hear her voice, really hear it, as she begged me to go on this trip. I hear the way she lingered on his name. In my mind, she rushes over the other names, not caring whether she sees them again or not.

She didn't even try to hide it.

Who knew I'd end up with someone just like my whore of a mother.

And when she called riding shotgun, her eyes lit up brighter than the fucking sun. I watch it play out in my mind, and this time I see the soft smile on his lips, see the way he leers at her.

Fucking Ian.

Kerry sits forward, craning her neck to see the road. She leans toward me, peering out between the seats and stealing my view of Ariella's betrayal. "Shut up, you guys," she tells the harlot and the casanova. "It wasn't that bad."

But I missed what they were laughing about.

Beside me, Jake laughs at his wife. "It really was."

She reaches over me to lightly smack his knee. Confined as we are, she hits my knee too, and I barely suppress a glare.

"Oh, sorry, Kurt," she says. Briefly, she leans her head against my shoulder in a sorry excuse for an apology, and her long brown hair tickles my arm. "See what you guys made me do!" she shoots at Jake. "You made me smack Kurt!"

Ariella's eyes dart upward, meeting mine in the rearview mirror. Dark eyes pulled tight with worry, she holds my gaze.

Is she afraid for Kerry?

People don't usually hit me and get away with it.

But she doesn't know that yet.

I hold myself in check, clenching my jaw. My hands ball up in my lap, but I cross my arms, tucking tight fists under my elbows.

Still staring at me, Kerry asks, "Are you okay?"

Ariella turns to look at me, waves of black hair spilling over the armrest. Long, silky tresses swirl over Ian's arm, and his eyes tear away from the road for a quick glance at her. His eyes sparkle in the waning sunlight, and the corners of his lips lift into a wistful smile.

My stomach sours.

"Kurt?" Kerry prompts, stealing my attention away from the philanderer in the front seat. Her crisp blue eyes stare into mine, edged with concern.

"I'm fine," I say, voice tight. "Just carsick. Always happens in little cars."

She accepts my lie, but when I look forward, Ariella's brows reach for each other, huddling in confusion. I've never been carsick in my life, and she knows it. I'm not that weak.

"Sorry, man," Ian says over his shoulder. "This is a pretty bumpy road. That probably doesn't help."

A deep breath puffs out my chest as I stare hard at Ariella.

"Do you… need to switch seats?" she offers, but I hear her reluctance.

After all, why would she want to give up her seat next to *Ian*?

"Oh, no," I answer quickly. "I'll be fine."

Her lips purse as she considers me, but only for an instant.

Ian taps her knee with the back of his hand, and she turns forward, not even sparing me a second thought. "We're here," he says.

Everyone else stares out the windows at the rickety old farmhouse and the shitty barn behind it. They gape and chatter excitedly about the murders that happened here in the early 1900s and the ghosts rumored to haunt the place.

But I stare at the lecher moving in on *my* woman. Blond scruff decorates his chin and his short blond hair is a mess.

Yet, she thinks she'll leave me for him?

I shake my head.

I'll be second to none.

Chapter 1
Ariella

The day before

"I don't see why you even want to go," Kurt moans from the next room.

But I keep packing, stuffing a second pair of jeans and a battery pack for my phone into my open suitcase. "Come on, Kurt. You know I love haunted places. And I haven't seen Ian or Jake or Tori in so long."

I tuck my brand-new EMF meter into the front pocket. Excitement buzzes through me, and I dig in my heels, determined not to let him spoil this for me.

"Besides," I say, "it's been forever since we all went on a trip. And Ian just graduated culinary school. This is supposed to be a celebration."

Sinking onto the couch with a groan, Kurt mumbles, "Yeah, that *really* makes me want to go. You should just stay. Ian can celebrate like a normal person and go out to eat or something."

"You know, you don't *have* to go," I remind him. I zip my suitcase, glancing around my bedroom to make sure I haven't forgotten anything. "I'll just see you on Monday when I get back."

Truth be told, I could use the space…

And I really do want to see Ian. It's been way too long.

I stuff down the feelings I know Ian doesn't have for me and try to focus on what's important. Packing… and deciding whether it's worth it to keep putting up with Kurt.

"What, so you're going to go without me? And be up there with all those guys… without me? Yeah, that'll go so well. I basically *have* to go."

Anger surges through me, and I pull in a deep breath, trying to calm myself.

Not this shit again…

I do everything I can not to take the bait, not to justify his possessiveness with a response, but my temper gets the best of me. He's worn my nerves thin with this crap, so I stomp to the door of my bedroom.

"There are so many things wrong with what you just said." I carefully keep my hands from balling into fists. "First of all, there's going to be more girls than guys. Second, and way more importantly, do you *really* not trust me? Have I *ever* given you reason not to?"

He sits quietly, scrolling through random crap on his phone, and I think myself the victor. Hoping he'll see how much of an ass he's being, I turn back to my bedroom.

But under his breath, he mumbles, "Maybe not that I know of…"

Another deep breath lifts my chest, and I clench my jaw. Hefting my suitcase from my bed with a little more force than is strictly necessary, I carry it out to the living room. I squeeze past the couch, banging the corners of the suitcase on the wall and hating how small my apartment is.

"Fine," Kurt says, still scrolling. His dark hair hangs loose as he peers closer at his phone, blocking his face from my view. "I guess I'll go. Get out of the city for a bit."

Oh great... Now he agrees. Just because he doesn't want me around other guys.

Sure, he's not all wrong. If I had a chance, I'd be with Ian. But I wouldn't cheat, for fuck's sake.

"Ok," I say, settling my luggage near the door. "Shouldn't you go home and pack, then?"

Please, go home. I need some time to myself.

"Nah, I'll pack after work tomorrow."

Groaning internally, I remind him that we need to leave as soon as we get out of work. I'm even leaving work early tomorrow because I want there to be some daylight left when we get there.

"You just can't wait to get rid of me, can you?" In a low voice, he adds, "Gonna have someone else over?" His head tips, and his eyebrows jolt up in a burst of attitude.

I stare at Kurt with my jaw hanging open.

Desperately, I try to remember what I ever saw in him. Brief flashes of laughing over memes and the heat of a budding relationship are quickly overshadowed by the bitterness that has seeped in over the past seven months. What I once thought was attentive passion has long since spoiled.

"Kurt," I say, voice carefully controlled. "We've talked about this before. I won't put up with this crap any longer. This weekend is your last chance to get your shit together."

I don't care that your mom left your dad for someone else. I'm not her. Don't take your shit out on me.

I bite my tongue, keeping that last bit to myself, though only barely. Squaring my shoulders, I glare at him with one raised eyebrow.

He looks up from his phone, finally, and something about the twitch in his jaw unsettles me. Darkness moves in his eyes, but I know he's just trying to intimidate me.

But I'm fucking done.

I hold my ground.

Rising to his feet, he shoves his phone in his pocket and strolls toward me. Nerves coil tight in my gut, writhing like snakes and begging me to open the door to the hall and run. But I won't give him the satisfaction.

His gaze holds mine, unwavering and unblinking. Stopping just a foot away, he stares down at me. "Guess I'd better go pack, then."

Stepping past me, he jerks the door open. He disappears into the hall, slamming the door as he leaves.

Shaking with what I tell myself is rage, not fear, I lock my door. Wandering into my room, I snatch my phone up from the nightstand. The little indicator flashes blue, and I smile when I see a new message from Ian.

"Have you read anything more about the house we're going to?"

"No. I've been a little…" I type, hesitating. I cast my mind over the evening and finish the text with "busy."

Before I even swipe the menu down to see what other notifications await me, he replies. "So… You haven't seen pictures of the basement, then? Man, what are you even doing? I thought you were a Ghost Hunter. Lol. Shouldn't you be scoping out the best places to set up your new gear?"

Despite everything that just happened, I smile. "Lol. It's this little thing called delegation. You know, that thing they taught us in all those business classes… You already did the work."

"Wow. So I'm just your little errand boy, now?"

My heart stutters, but I remind myself that this is just Ian. He's always been like this. And the one time we kissed, drunk as we may have been, nothing came of it.

"Errand boy… Secretary… Whatever you want to call it. Lol."

In an instant, I get a reply. "Ouch."

I laugh, staring at the little picture of him beside his name. The bright sunlight of our graduation day sparkles on the blond scruff coating his strong jaw. Back before he decided to really pursue his dream of being a chef. His blue eyes dance with laughter.

Before I can type a response, a new message pops up. "Want to see pictures of the basement?"

"Did you save them or something?" I send, settling onto my bed with a smile on my face.

"Um… Duh."

"Weirdo."

"So… Do you want to see them?"

“Um… Duh.”

Chapter 2
Ian

Traffic swells around me, swallowing my little car. Yet another red light brings me to a stop, and taxis pull up on both sides of me, wrapping me in yellow. A motorcycle drives alongside me, splitting lanes as they squeeze between me and the cab.

But I don't feel the customary surge of anxiety at having a motorcycle so close to my car.

Instead, excitement surges through me. The light turns green, unleashing me onto another street, getting me just a little closer to Ari.

The motorcycle weaves, pulling ahead and leaving me behind in the maze of cars. Turning off the main road, I head toward her apartment, delving into a slightly run-down neighborhood. The road opens around me, clearing of cars, and I drive just a little faster than I should.

But as her building comes into view, I remind myself.

She has a boyfriend.

And you have to be nice to this guy. They've been together a while, now. She must be serious about him.

The thought crushes me. Despite all my efforts to move on while she's been with Kurt, despite every attempt I've made at distancing myself from her… nothing works.

I still love her.

Our one kiss flashes through my mind, foggy beneath the layers of alcohol that coated my mind that night. Far too sloppy, nothing like what I always imagined our first kiss would be like, it haunts me.

I still see the spark in her eyes, the one that sobriety and the light of dawn convinced me I just imagined. I still feel her hands, so gentle as they touched my face.

But awkwardness fell over us the next day, harsh and brutal.

Because…

Did she really want to kiss me?

Or was she just drunk?

Again, I hate how I just stood there, staring at her, stunned. I hate the embarrassment that bloomed over her cheeks, clearly visible in the too-bright lights of the dorm hallway.

Sighing, I remind myself just how useless it is to go over it, again and again. Pulling up outside her building, nestling my car into a parallel spot, I tell myself again.

She has a boyfriend.

If she felt anything for me then, she moved on.

After putting the car in neutral, I set the parking brake and grab my phone to send her a message. "I'm outside."

It registers as "seen" almost immediately, and my heart bursts into butterflies.

Get a grip, man.

But I leap from my car as soon as the coast is clear of oncoming traffic, rushing around to lean against it to wait for her. Feigning nonchalance, I check my email, finding one from my new boss telling me what to expect on Monday.

I also find a message from my dad, asking if I'm coming for a visit this weekend. I start to respond, but my fingers stall out on the screen.

I lose track of myself, trying to figure out what to say. I already told him that I'm going out of town with Ari and everyone to celebrate. I told him I have to be back late Sunday night for work on Monday.

But he has yet to congratulate me on finishing culinary school.

And he's made his views on staying friends with Ari crystal clear.

In my mind, I hear him tell me to stop torturing myself, over and again. But the door to her apartment building opens and closes, pulling my eyes away from my phone.

And there she is.

All my careful preparations to hold myself together go out the window. Long, dark hair hangs in gorgeous waves, cascading past her shoulders. Her lips part in a beautiful smile, painted a dark red to draw the eye.

And it works.

My gaze traces her lips, recalling the way they felt against mine, if only briefly, last year.

Dark eyes grapple for my attention, sparkling in the late afternoon sun. I pull in a deep breath, smiling wide.

"Ari…" I whisper.

She drops her suitcase and rushes forward.

And I'm helpless, moving to meet her. I throw my arms around her, pulling her in tight. My fingers wrap in silky black hair, and I breathe, "God, I missed you."

Too late, I realize my slip. Blushing, I bury my face in her hair to hide.

How did I think I could stay away from her?

What the fuck made me think that would help?

Her arms tighten around me, and my skin tingles, aching for more.

"Yeah, well, someone had classes and exams and work and a bunch of other shit to do…" she says. Her tone is so light, so gentle.

But guilt spreads through me.

Because I know I lied to her.

I've spent so much time just twiddling my thumbs this semester, going to parties to try to forget her.

"Fuck classes…" I mumble, releasing her. My arms revolt against the motion, but I keep them carefully under my control, dropping them to my sides.

"You can say that now that you're done with them," she says, laughing easily.

Turning, she reaches for her suitcase, but I step forward. "I don't think so. I've got it."

I take it easily and extend a hand to take Kurt's luggage. "What's up, Kurt?" I say, carefully monitoring my tone. Every syllable, each inflection is weighed and measured for politeness.

And I hate it.

Kurt mumbles a greeting, awkward and tense, and insists that he can carry his luggage.

"Shotgun," Ari yells. She jumps into the passenger seat quickly, and a stupid flutter of hope rushes through me.

She wants to sit next to me…

But I chastise myself for the thought.

"So, what have you been up to?" I ask.

But Kurt barely answers.

Okay then…

I slam the trunk shut, and we climb into the car. Ari already has our ghost hunting playlist fired up, and I smile at her.

Chapter 3
Ariella

My phone lights up on the counter, showing a message from Ian. "I'm outside."

My heart skips a beat, but I suppress the smile that tries so hard to creep over my face. Maintaining a normal tone of voice, I say, "He's here."

"Awesome," Kurt says from the next room. A bitter undercurrent seethes beneath his words.

Sighing, I slide my phone into my back pocket, yet again lamenting the fake pockets on the front of my jeans. I roll my eyes at Kurt, granting myself that little bit of rudeness before I turn around.

I scan my little apartment, making sure I haven't left anything out that needs put away for the weekend. I run through a mental checklist, hoping not to forget anything. Satisfied, I meander the short distance from my kitchen to my front door and lift my suitcase.

But Kurt stands awkwardly in the door to my bedroom, staring into the dark room.

"Kurt? Are you ready?"

He stands for a moment longer, and a muscle in his jaw twitches. But finally, he turns. "Ready as I'm going to be."

He grabs his suitcase and follows me out. I lock the door, hoping no one will break in while I'm away.

A weird feeling in my stomach tells me things won't be the same when I come back here, and for a second, I consider asking my dad to check in on the place. But I push the notion away, dismissing it as silly.

Besides, it's such a long drive into the city. I couldn't ask him to do that.

After all, the only thing that might change is that I might not be with Kurt anymore after this weekend.

A little thrill sparks through me, and I wonder if my decision is already made.

We make our way down three flights of stairs, lugging our bags and sweating in the summer heat. Finally, the stairs end, and I rush through the lobby, passing mailboxes aplenty. The door opens easily, offering no protest as I push through to the sidewalk.

And there he is.

Leaning against his little blue car, Ian stares down at his phone. His short blond hair shines in the sun, and his dark t-shirt clings to his lean form.

He looks up, blue eyes catching sight of me. With a sharp intake of breath, a smile breaks over his lips. "Ari…" he breathes.

Rushing forward, I drop my suitcase on the sidewalk, and Ian throws his arms around me.

He squeezes tight, whispering, "God, I missed you," into my hair.

My arms tighten around him, and I do my best to ignore the heat pooling within me and the flock of butterflies swarming in my chest. "Yeah, well, someone had classes and exams and work and a bunch of other shit to do…" I tease.

"Fuck classes…" he mumbles, but he releases me.

"You can say that now that you're done with them," I say, laughing despite the pain of not being in his arms. Turning, I reach for my suitcase, but Ian steps forward.

"I don't think so. I've got it." He takes it and even extends a hand to take Kurt's luggage. "What's up, Kurt?" he says, tone perfectly polite and even.

A bit too even? Maybe controlled?

But I chide myself for reading into it.

Kurt returns the greeting by insisting that he can carry his own luggage.

"Shotgun," I yell, running for the passenger seat while they're distracted because I know Ian will be driving. It's his car, after all. Climbing in, I connect the radio to my phone and select the same playlist I always play when we go somewhere haunted.

I'll start it over when we pick up Jake and Kerry, giving them the full effect. The song "Book of the Flies" by Projekt F starts playing, and instantly, excitement builds within me.

My mind floods with our previous trips during college, back when Ian was studying business alongside me. Old insane asylums and houses plagued by murder. Ghost towns and hotels with rumors of possessions.

In my mind, I hear hundreds of creaking floorboards and remember lights that switched on and off by themselves. An eerie scream wafts through my memories, calling out to us from a dark church we visited junior year.

Ian slams the trunk of the car, and I jump. Laughing at myself, I fall back into the present.

The doors open, and Kurt slides into the back. Climbing into the driver's seat, Ian glances at the radio and smiles.

Chapter 4
Ian

After a couple hours, the GPS directs us through our final turn, sending us down a pocked dirt road. It winds around a lake and several fields. I slow and swerve to miss as many of the potholes as I can, trying to spare Kerry any carsickness.

Ari laughs beside me, tipping her head back as she does. Her tan skin glitters in the waning sunlight, and her eyes sparkle beautifully. We hit a pothole that spans the full width of the road, and her arm bumps mine on the armrest, sending warmth tingling through me.

"I still can't believe you got on that freaking bar, Kerry," she teases.

Jake lets out a sharp bark of laughter as the memory washes over him, and Kerry tries to defend herself. I laugh along with them, but only bits and pieces of the conversation filter through the haze of wanting Ari's arm to rest against mine again.

Guilt lands heavily in my chest because I know she's with Kurt. And he's right there. But her arm bumps mine again, and a rush of heat chases the guilt away.

"Why did you think it was a good idea to climb up there, anyway?" Jake asks. He smiles wide in the rearview, leaning forward to peer past Kurt.

"I didn't want to be *on* the bar. I wanted behind it. That's where the alcohol was…" Kerry says, drawing the words out on a giggle.

"Yeah, that worked out *real well*," Ari says. She tips her head back, covering her mouth as she laughs deeply.

When she puts her arm back down, it presses against mine. Heat surges through me, and this time, she barely pulls away. Every little bump and shimmy brushes her skin against mine.

"Shut up, you guys," Kerry says. "It wasn't that bad."

I shoot a glance over my shoulder with eyebrows raised. "Not that bad?"

Ari peers back at her. "Kerry, you puked on the whole crowd. That's pretty bad."

"It really was," Jake teases.

Leaning forward, Kerry smacks Jake's knee. "Oh, sorry, Kurt," she says. "See what you guys made me do! You made me smack Kurt!"

And for the first time in nearly twenty minutes, I notice how quiet Kurt is. He sits, ramrod straight, clenching his jaw. For a moment, I feel bad for talking about college so much, since he wasn't there.

But he doesn't say anything.

A little muscle in his jaw twitches, barely visible in stolen glances at the rearview. But a deep unease settles in my stomach.

It worsens when Ari grows quiet, staring at him in the mirror.

"Are you okay?" Kerry asks.

Ari turns in her seat to face him, leaning over the armrest. Long, silky tresses tickle my skin, and my eyes dart to her. My lips lift into a smile, despite the strange feeling in the pit of my stomach.

"Kurt?" Kerry asks again.

Ari still stares at him.

I slow the car down, shifting to a lower gear. Just in case. I'm not sure what I'm preparing for, but my gut tells me to prepare.

But finally, Kurt speaks. "I'm fine," he says, voice far too tight to actually be fine. "Just carsick. Always happens in little cars."

And suddenly, I feel worse for enjoying every bump in the road, simply because it brushed Ari's arm against mine. "Sorry, man. This is a pretty bumpy road," I say, briefly glancing over my shoulder. "That probably doesn't help."

"Do you…" Ari begins, drawing the words out, "need to switch seats?"

My heart drops at the prospect of sharing the front with Kurt instead of her.

But…

Did she sound… reluctant?

Internally, I kick myself.

Stop getting your hopes up.

"Oh, no. I'll be fine," Kurt says.

And then, I see it.

Peeking out from a shady patch in the field, an old grey farmhouse awaits. Moss and vines cling to every side but one, nearly consuming the place. White shutters hang on every window, but half of them tilt to the side.

It looks just like any rundown old house. It certainly doesn't look like it played host to four vicious murders and a suicide about a hundred years ago.

Off in the distance, perched between sparse trees, the barn looms.

The barn.

The place where the victims were taken after they grew weak, after they withered in the basement of the house for nearly two weeks. The place where they were tortured and killed.

I tap Ari's knee with the back of my hand, desperate to share this first impression with her. She turns forward, gazing at me with a smile on her face.

"We're here," I say, inclining my head toward the old house.

She turns to look at the place, just as a curtain moves in an upstairs window.

Gasping, she grabs my arm. "Did you see that?"

Excitement bubbles within me, and my skin tingles at her touch. "Want to set up your EMF meter there?"

"Fuck yeah!" She bounces in her seat, chomping at the bit to get into the place.

I turn the car and coast into the weed-riddled driveway.

"Which one do you think it was?" I ask. "That'd be… What, the master bedroom?" I try to recall the floorplan, piecing it together with the sight before me.

"Oh my god," Ari starts, staring straight at me. "Do you think it was him? Do you think he's mad that people are coming to stay, again?"

Slowing to a halt in the driveway, I slip the car into neutral and say, "Maybe that'll make him talk to us."

Kerry squeals in the backseat, and Ari leans over me to peer up at the house. The luscious floral scent of her shampoo wafts up to tickle my nose, and I smile, despite myself.

"Only one way to find out," Jake says, climbing out of the car before I even set the parking brake.

But Kurt never says a word.

Chapter 5
Ariella

Slowly spinning in place, I glance at the turn of the century kitchen. A wood-burning cast-iron stove sits proudly in one corner, and a massive ice chest stands in another. Both sparkle despite their age.

You can't even tell Theodore Alton hit his wife over the head in this very room, right before dragging her to the basement to starve for a couple weeks.

I run my hands over the old worktable, wondering what was going through his head when he did it. What could have pushed him so far? Glancing at the floor, clean of blood after nearly a hundred years, I wonder if she saw him coming, if she fought.

Rumors of possession flitted through the town, but the papers of the time dismissed them quickly, calling him a vicious madman. And on all accounts, he seemed fully in control of himself.

At least... as far as possession is concerned.

He certainly lost control, but no evil spirits were controlling him.

I close my eyes, listening to the house, feeling the way it moves. Old houses always move, creaking with a life of their own. But I need to be able to sort out the sounds of the house from the sounds of our potential housemates.

True to form, a board creaks behind me, but not of its own accord. I turn around quickly, only to find Kurt dragging his suitcase behind him. He drops it beside mine at the door and casts a dubious glance over the place.

Rustic furnishings perch in corners, waiting for the former occupants to return. An old painting hangs above the couch, varnish so yellowed with age that the portrait, likely once a stunning visage, now appears sinister and cloudy. A massive fireplace yawns hungrily, waiting for things to burn.

Does it remember the body parts Theodore Alton once burned within it?

Preserved in shadow boxes on the mantle, the fragments of bone that the police fished out of the ash beg me to look them over.

But Kurt merely groans.

"Let me guess," he says. "That fireplace is how we're going to stay warm?"

"Probably," Ian says, stepping in behind Kurt. He smiles at me, then adds, "That and blankets."

Briefly, I regret waiting to break it off with Kurt. I could've cozied up to Ian under a bunch of old blankets, maybe tried to kiss him, again.

But then I see him, see the way he stared at me blankly when I kissed him last year. Some slurred apology fell from my lips that night, begging his forgiveness and hoping it wouldn't mess up our friendship. And through every word I said, he just stood there, staring at me. The humiliation washes over me for the millionth time.

Could I put myself through that, again?

"Does this *hole* at least have plumbing?" Kurt asks, calling me back to the present.

I stifle a laugh.

A preserved farmhouse from the early 1900s? Indoor plumbing?

Ian scrunches his eyes and tips his head to the side. "Not quite."

Kurt pulls in a long, slow breath.

For a second, I feel bad for not thinking to tell him.

But what did he expect?

And I did show him pictures…

Did he not pay attention to them? The outhouse is pretty hard to miss.

"Well," Ian says, rubbing his hands together and easing past the awkward hush. He clears the distance between us quickly. Opening the icebox, he finds a massive block inside. He opens the other doors and finds the groceries he emailed the owners about. "Let's get dinner started, shall we?"

As Ian pulls fresh vegetables and a pack of chicken breasts from the ice chest, Jake and Kerry meander into the hall beyond the living room, toting their luggage along with them. They drop the heavy things in one of the bedrooms with a couple of soft thuds. Drawers open as they unpack.

Kerry's voice carries toward us. "Damn it…"

My eyes lift to the hall. "Everything okay?" I call out.

"Yeah, I just… Forgot something at home."

Kurt settles onto the antique floral print couch, apparently content to wait for dinner. Barely visible through the doorway, he pulls his phone from his pocket and groans about the lack of cell service.

I try to suppress an eye roll, but it slips through.

And of course, Ian catches it. A smile spreads over his lips as he turns to the kitchen piano, the only set of cabinets in here.

Was I supposed to see that smile?

Somehow, it seems like he meant to hide it, and a guilty little thrill slips over my spine. Butterflies play in my stomach.

But I force myself back to reality.

He only sees me as a friend.

That's how it's always been.

"What did you forget?" I ask, listening to Kerry's soft footsteps as they carry her toward me. "I might have something you can borrow."

She steps back into the living room, long brown hair swaying behind her as she walks. Laughing, she says, "I'm not about to borrow your underwear. I'm sure they have a general store in town."

Laughter consumes the kitchen, filling Ian and I. Kerry joins in, but Kurt stays silent, analyzing Kerry's curvy figure.

"How did you forget underwear?" I ask.

"I don't know. I always forget *something*."

Jake appears behind her, nodding vehemently. Smiling, he mouths, "Always."

"Can we borrow your car to run to town, Ian?" Kerry asks. "I was going to call Tori and Sarah and ask them to pick some up for me, but I don't have any service."

Nodding, Ian tosses her the keys. "Here you go. I'd tell you not to let Jake drive, but he can't drive stick anyway."

"God, this again…" Jake shakes his head, laughing all the while.

I start to put the food back in the ice chest, but Kerry tells me not to wait on them.

"Go ahead and eat. Just save us some."

And with that, they leave me alone with Ian in the kitchen. Stepping up to the worktable, I open the package of chicken. Ian steps up, settling two cutting boards and two knives beside me before returning to the cabinet for a skillet.

He brings it over, placing it on the table along with a small sack of potatoes. His hand finds the small of my back, surprising me, and heat rushes through my veins.

"Excuse me, just gotta…" he says, leaning across the table to grab the vegetables he set out.

I laugh nervously as color rises over my chest and neck on waves of heat. My eyes flit to the doorway, hoping Kurt isn't looking. But he isn't on the couch anymore.

Footsteps tell me he's skirting the room, drawing closer.

And for some reason, that makes me even more nervous.

Pulling the vegetables closer to his cutting board, Ian stands up straight and removes his hand from my back. He peels potatoes carefully, arm bumping mine as he works.

Sliding one of the cutting boards closer, I place a chicken breast upon it. "Alright, how do you want these cut?"

Kurt steps into the doorway, eyeing us carefully.

"Uh, fillet it, please."

I butcher the first one, and Ian laughs.

"Okay, maybe you should peel potatoes."

Laughing, I roll my eyes at him. "Are you saying I'm bad at this?"

"Oh, no. Never." His blue eyes twinkle with mirth. "Just… inexperienced."

"Yeah, that's code for, 'you suck at this.'"

Laughing, I admit defeat and set the knife down. After cleaning my hands at the water basin, I take my place at the table. Ian moves to the stove, pulling firewood from the stack next to it. As I peel potatoes, he starts a fire.

Kurt watches us carefully, though something about his expression seems off. He steps up to the worktable, still silent, and a hush falls over the room.

"Want to help?" Ian asks, returning to the table.

Kurt shakes his head. "Cooking isn't really my thing."

Silence falls upon us once more, and I squirm beneath it. "How many of these do you need me to peel?" I ask, desperate to fill the air.

"Four," Ian answers. "They need cubed. And could you cut up the onions, garlic, and tomatoes, too?"

I stare at him, waiting for him to tell me how many of each.

"The recipe is on my phone," he says, sighing dramatically, but a laugh quickly follows.

And suddenly, Kurt joins the world, again, reaching for Ian's phone. He taps the screen, and when the keypad appears, waiting for the password, he looks up at Ian expectantly.

I scrunch my brows, wondering what's gotten into him.

Ian sets his knife down and reaches for his phone with his clean hand. "I got it. No worries."

Chapter 6
Kurt

Ariella does a poor job of filleting the chicken breast, and Ian offers to switch with her.

Did she want him to show her how to do it? Like all the big strong men in romance movies show women how to do things? From behind, with arms around them.

Bitterness swells within me, even as Ariella laughs. She rolls her eyes at Ian, far more playful than she's been with me in months. "Are you saying I'm bad at this?" she asks.

"Oh, no. Never. Just…" Ian's eyes twinkle, practically undressing her as he says, "inexperienced."

"Yeah, that's code for, 'you suck at this.'" Ariella laughs again, setting her knife down.

My jaw clenches as I watch them.

They've probably been having sex behind my back for months. Every time she's said she wanted me to go home, every time she didn't want me to sleep over… I bet she was with him.

She cleans her hands at the basin, but no amount of soap could ever wash away the filth of what she's been doing with him. Ian glances at her as he moves to the stove, starting a fire within it that could never rival the heat scorching my veins right now.

Ariella glances at me as she begins peeling potatoes, and I step closer. Staring into her eyes, I try to figure out why she would've brought me along this weekend.

Maybe to flaunt her adultery, to rub it in my face.

Does it make her feel powerful?

I seethe beneath the notion of her twisting me to fit her sick needs. Then, I remember her words, so casual as she finished packing for the trip.

"You know, you don't have to go," she said, and now her voice floats through my mind, an eerie reminder of just how brazen she is. "I'll just see you on Monday when I get back."

She practically screamed her intentions.

She wanted me to stay in the city so she could have sex with Ian, all weekend long.

And of course, none of her shitty friends would've said a word about it to me.

Because I'm not in their fucked up little group.

I glance at Ian, crouching near the stove as he feeds firewood into it. For a moment, I wonder what it would feel like to push him, to bash his head against that cast-iron monstrosity.

To feel his skull give way.

To watch his hair ignite and his skin melt in the heat of the fire.

The poetic justice of him dying by the very fire he stokes, even now, warms my heart.

But he rises, returning to the table and standing far too close to Ariella. "Want to help?" he asks, holding my gaze.

I shake my head, making every effort to conceal my rage. "Cooking isn't really my thing."

He shrugs and smiles, dropping his gaze to the chicken breasts still in need of butchering. Setting to work, he slices through them easily, occasionally glancing at Ariella's busy hands.

I'll rip that smile off your face if you don't keep your eyes off her…

"How many of these do you need me to peel?" Ariella asks.

"Four. They need cubed," Ian says. "And could you cut up the onions, garlic, and tomatoes, too?"

Ariella stares at him, eyes lingering far too long on his face.

How bold can she be?

"The recipe is on my phone," Ian says with an overly drawn-out sigh, baiting her, begging her to flirt back. He even laughs, jabbing at me with how little he cares for my presence.

I grab his phone, sliding it toward me on the table. I tap the screen and stare at him, daring him not to give me the password.

Ariella looks at me with eyes wide, but Ian merely scrunches his brows. Setting his knife down, he slides the phone back toward him. "I got it. No worries."

Spinning it quickly to face him, laying his salmonella-coated left hand on the cutting board, he enters, 381991. My mouth falls open, and I stare at him.

Because I know those numbers.

Ariella's birthday is his password?

Is he fucking joking?

He scrolls over a typed note, having left the recipe open when he last locked his phone. His eyes lift to mine for just a second, and he flinches before the intensity of my gaze. A small flicker of satisfaction moves through me, and I raise one eyebrow.

Apparently putting two and two together, he pulls in a deep breath.

He knows I've figured out their little secret. It's so goddamn obvious, anyway. How stupid do they think I am?

And then, I realize why I haven't seen Ian as much, lately. I used to think she was just hanging out with him less because she wanted to be with me instead.

But now, I know.

He's been pulling her away. He's hated me from the start, and he wanted her to hang out with him away from me.

I seethe, and my stare intensifies.

Setting his phone next to Ariella, he goes back to work. His eyes widen momentarily, and he mouths something down at the cutting board.

Ariella turns the phone, leaning over it to read the recipe. But she scrolls up a little too fast, and the app closes.

Ian's home screen lays before me, blaring a picture of him with Ariella. They stand together in front of a shitty, rundown little church. His arm hangs casually around her shoulders, and they beam into the camera.

"Aw, I love that picture!" Ariella says, smiling at Ian.

"Me, too," he answers, and I almost puke.

"Remember that weird scream we heard that night?" Ari asks, pulling the recipe up quickly, navigating his phone far too easily not to have done it a million times. "I swear, out of every trip we've taken, that was the closest we got to recording a ghost."

"If only someone had been a little quicker with their phone…" Ian teases.

I wonder what kept her hands too busy to get her phone out for the one thing they supposedly do together...

"I know! I'm so mad at myself over that," she says.

But dear Ariella, you could never be angry enough after all you've put me through.

Ian gathers the chicken breasts, all freshly filleted, and lays them out in the pan. Glancing at the one Ari cut, he laughs and says, "You guys can have the pretty ones. I'll eat that one."

I bet you fucking will...

Turning on my heel, I stomp out of the room. My feet lead me through the hall, and I pick a door at random. It opens to reveal stone stairs, and I rush down them, leaving the door open in my wake.

The chill of the cellar wraps around me as I descend.

Chapter 7
Ian

Kurt stomps out of the room and down the hall. A door jerks open, squealing loudly in the silent house, and his footsteps thud down to the basement.

Ari stares after him, gazing at the empty hallway. Her hands still, falling onto the cutting board with a thud.

But I drop my gaze.

He saw my password. I know he knows it's her birthday.

And the picture…

A sick feeling seeps into me.

He has to have guessed how I feel.

I quickly lay out the remainder of the chicken breasts within the pan and clean my hands. But they tremble in the water.

I have to tell him I won't intervene. I'm sure he's smart enough to see how I feel about Ari, especially now. But…

If she's happy, I'll leave it alone.

My stomach turns at the thought of having to talk to Kurt about anything, especially *this*. Something about the look in his eyes when he saw my password and the picture chilled me to the bone.

I'm sure it's nothing. He was just mad.

And he has every right to be.

Turning back to the worktable, I gather up all the spices I need and set to work seasoning and spreading vegetables in the pan. As my hands go through the motions, I try desperately not to overthink every aspect of the coming conversation with Kurt.

But my mind wanders, showing me a million insults he could throw at me, a million ways I could say it just wrong enough to make the whole situation worse.

A million ways he could turn Ari against me.

My blood runs cold at the thought.

Only when I place the last of the cut vegetables in the pan do I realize how long Ari and I have worked in silence. Some strange thud echoes up to us from the basement, drawing Ari's attention.

She settles the knife on the cutting board and wipes her hands clean. A scowl darkens her beautiful features as she says, "I should check on him, figure out what's gotten into him."

But I know.

He's mad at me. He's jealous.

As soon as I saw Ari, I just fell right back into my old rapport with her. Laughing and smiling like we always used to. All the glances I told myself to avoid, all the joy at little accidental touches, the butterflies…

Everything I warned myself against before coming here…

It all rushed back.

And now, Kurt knows.

I want to tell Ari not to go down there. He's going to say something, I know it, and I don't want her to find out from him. But I let her go.

Our one kiss floats through my mind, and again, I see her stare at me, embarrassed and apologizing. I watch her rush away, finding Kerry to drink some more as I stand paralyzed and dumbfounded.

Now, I watch her walk away, seeking the man she's replaced me with.

And I say nothing.

Dread pools within me, anticipating some deep look of disappointment to mar her face when she comes back into the kitchen. As I pick up the knife to finish cutting vegetables, I can almost hear her saying, "I just don't feel that way about you. You're my best friend."

A million times, my mind speaks in her voice, calling that one kiss a drunken mistake, something that never should've happened. I can picture her face as she says it, lips barely parting as she whispers the words that'll shatter my heart. I can already see the sympathy glowing in her big brown eyes.

Taking a deep breath, I try to steel myself against what I know will happen as soon as she comes back upstairs. Chopping away, I finish prepping dinner. Meticulously placing it all in the pan, trying desperately to make it presentable, I fidget with cubed onions and tomatoes.

I look over my work and clean my hands. I check the stove, shoving a couple more logs into the fire. Meandering back to the worktable, I reach for the cast-iron skillet.

But downstairs, Kurt shouts, "BULLSHIT!"

My eyes jerk to the hallway, and my hand stills on the handle of the skillet.

And suddenly, my feet are moving, carrying me toward the basement.

Chapter 8
Ariella

My heart races, and my stomach jumps into my throat as I pad gently down the stairs. But what the hell am I nervous about?

He's just being an asshole.

Again.

And suddenly, I'm not as nervous. Anger courses through me, steeling my nerves. Remembering the scowl on Kurt's face when he saw the picture on Ian's phone, the one that made my stupid heart do a little dance, I clench my fists.

Because I know Ian doesn't have feelings for me. Whether I wish he did or not, he doesn't.

We're just friends. Friends have pictures of their friends on their phones.

I told myself that very thing when I saw the picture, quelling the stupid lingering hope that maybe someday it would work.

Now, I prepare to say it to Kurt, voicing my anti-Ian mantra to tamp down his jealousy.

Stepping into the basement, lit up by a too-bright, battery-powered LED work light hanging in the center of the room, I stare at Kurt. Off to the side, he paces the length of the room, staring at the floor as he moves closer, then away.

Beside me, the heavy door to the cell hangs open. A solid metal bar rests in a glass case near the door and metal rungs stick out from the wall, but they haven't held that bar, pinning the door shut, in nearly a century. Lit by another LED work light, the room Theodore Alton starved his victims in waits.

Of course, Kurt came down here. He doesn't even care about this place.

I wanted to see this for the first time with Ian and everyone after dinner. Tori and Sarah aren't even here. Kerry and Jake won't be back for a while.

We always explore together. But he ruined that, too.

I stare at him, clenching my jaw.

I should've just broken up with him before we came here. Why the fuck did I give him another chance?

I stuff down the sympathy over his childhood, shoving away all the things about it that just don't add up. His cheating mother abandoning him. The weird scars on his back. His father's sudden death.

Again, I remind myself that he refuses to deal with his problems, that he puts them all on me.

I've given him plenty of chances. I should've just broken up with him.

But I didn't.

And now, I have to deal with this *for the rest of the weekend.*

"Kurt," I say, but he doesn't acknowledge me. Even when he comes closer, passing right by me, he doesn't see me.

He paces, back and forth, back and forth. His hands ball into fists in his hair, and he mumbles something.

A wave of concern sweeps through me, but something slick and greasy follows in its wake, settling deep in my gut. "Kurt?" I ask again, but this time, my voice breaks beneath the weight of his name.

Finally, just beside the staircase, he stops. His gaze deserts the floor, landing hard on me.

And I flinch before him.

He drops his hands to his side, and for a long moment, he stares at me. Anger quivers in the little muscles at the side of his jaw. His fingers tremble with it.

In only a few steps, he clears the distance between us, stepping between me and the stairs. "Now, you want to be with me, huh? You left him up there by himself to be with me. Oh, I'm so touched."

"What?" I ask.

I stare at him, confused. And some little voice in the back of my head tells me to go back upstairs, to squeeze past him and run.

But Kurt takes another step toward me, and my body goes rigid. The idea of movement deserts me, rooting me to the spot.

"Or did you come down here to fess up?" Kurt says, voice low and sinister.

My mind goes blank. One thought, and one thought only, trudges through the vast expanse.

Fess up for what?

But my tongue lies useless on the floor of my mouth. My eyebrows scrunch together, giving away my confusion.

"Don't play dumb, Ariella. It doesn't suit you." Dark brown eyes glare into mine. "You really thought I wouldn't figure it out? How stupid do you think I am?"

My mouth opens, finally moving, but no words come out. I shake my head feebly.

"I *know*. I know you've been sleeping with Ian. You stupid whore."

And for a moment, I find my voice. Anger surges through me, pushing the words out. "Excuse me?"

"Don't fucking pretend. I saw how you guys were looking at each other. I saw his phone and his fucking password. He had the goddamn *balls* to make it your birthday, just rubbing it in my face. Fucking prick," he spits.

My veins fill with ice as I watch something snap behind Kurt's eyes.

"We're just friends," I whisper.

"BULLSHIT!" Kurt shouts, shattering my frail nerves.

I jump, and he laughs. But the sound contains no mirth.

"You stupid bitch. You really thought you could get away with it. You even guilted me into coming here so you could fuck him in the next room. Did you really think I'd put up with that?"

"But… We're just friends, Kurt. We've never had sex." I try to keep my voice from faltering. But I fail.

Kurt slaps me, hard and fast.

Pain blossoms across my skull, and my eyes water. The floor slams into me before I realize I've fallen. My hand flies out, smacking into the doorframe of the cell. My ears ring, and a strange, solid pulse reverberates beneath them.

Ian's voice thunders out over the noise in my head. But I never saw him come down here, and I can't make out his words.

Darkness claims me.

Chapter 9
Ian

Rage coils tight within me, and my hands shake with it. Kurt's shout reverberates through my mind like a war drum, pulling me toward the stairs.

I may not know why he's yelling at Ari, but I know she deserves better.

So, I move faster, barreling down the stairs. The cold basement comes into view just in time for me to watch him slap Ari across the face.

And all I see is red.

She falls to the floor as I shout at him. Words form of their own volition, giving voice to the fury roiling in my gut, but I hardly notice what I say.

Careening into him, I throw a punch. But my furious descent and my battle cry warned him of my approach.

He ducks, catching only a glancing blow to the cheek.

Before I realize what's happening, before I can pull back for another punch, his fist slams into my stomach. Pain bursts through me, but he gives me no time to process it.

He rises, driving the top of his head into my chin, and I fly backward, only just managing to keep my feet underneath me. My eyes well up, stinging with tears, and my jaw aches. Disoriented, I sway on my feet.

But rage guides me. It pushes me toward him again.

Screaming out, I pull back to punch him, landing a slightly more solid blow to his face.

But he shoves me, taking advantage of my fragile balance.

I trip over Ari, landing in the cell.

As I struggle to my feet, Kurt heaves Ari's unconscious form into the cell with a grunt. He slams the door shut. Glass shatters beyond the door, and I hear the scrape of metal over wood. Then, the hollow clank of metal landing on metal.

Nearly falling, I leap over Ari and twist the doorknob. I push as hard as I can, but I'm too late. Only then do I remember the pictures of the basement and the bar that Kurt must have slid into place, locking us in here.

But for how long?

Suddenly, every glare since we left the city takes on new meaning, and I wonder just how much of a fucking psycho Kurt might actually be. Every little look, every gesture that I dismissed as being normal, telling myself that I was reading into it, that I was just jealous…

They all come back to bite me.

How many red flags did I ignore?

My gaze falls from the door, landing on Ari. I crawl over to her and pull her into my arms. A sick feeling slithers through my gut as I gaze at the red mark on her face.

Has he done this before?

Hatred wells within me, and I glare at the door.

Beyond it, Kurt paces. But only temporarily. He slams a fist on the door, hard and loud, and I jump. Ari jolts in my arms, wincing with the movement.

Again, Kurt slams his fist against the door, letting out a wild scream.

My blood runs cold.

Blinking awake, Ari stares at the door in horror. Objects smash into the wall, groaning as they crack and splinter. And suddenly, I'm thankful for the barrier between us and Kurt.

I wrap my arms around Ari, pulling her against me. She twists to face the door, leaning against me.

But Kurt stills, and silence falls beyond the door. Only the sound of my galloping heart and my ragged breathing fill my ears.

If he opens that door…

I prepare myself, knowing that if he comes in here, I have to do better. I just didn't expect him to be so good at fighting. True, it's never been something I sought out. I'm not exactly a pro.

But... Kurt dodged so easily. He knew exactly what to do.

When I hit him, it didn't even phase him.

And suddenly, I realize just how little I know about him and his past.

Sitting on the floor of a cell, waiting for him to come to his senses or devolve further into madness, my nerves wind tight. My breath comes in shallow gasps, and some of Ari's hair presses itself to my lips.

She holds herself still, rigid and tense in my arms. Her hands wrap around my forearms, squeezing tight. But her chest and back move with quick breaths.

Footsteps explode through the silence, echoing through the basement.

But they move toward the stairs.

Thudding upward, Kurt leaves us locked away. The door to the basement slams behind him, and the floorboards groan beneath his wiry frame as he moves through the house.

I piece the floorplan together in my memory, trying to pinpoint where he ended up.

The living room?

Maybe his and Ari's room? It's right beside it.

A teardrop lands on my arm, diverting my attention. A soft whimper chokes its way free of Ari's lips, and I tip her head back with one hand.

She doesn't meet my gaze, and a sharp lance of pain pierces my heart. Tears flow freely over her cheeks.

"Has he…" I try to swallow a lump in my throat, try to push words past it. Clearing my throat, I try again. "Has he done that before?"

This whole time, while I've been avoiding her... Has he been hitting her?

Guilt washes through me on waves of ice water, and my heart shrivels in my chest. Fury follows close behind, burning me alive.

But she shakes her head. "He's just…" She shakes her head again. "He's been a jerk. But… This was the first time."

Gathering her up, I pull Ari onto my lap. "It's the *last* time," I whisper. "I'll make sure he never does that, again. I swear it, Ari."

Even if it's the last thing I ever do.

Tears soak into my shirt, and she slides her arms around my waist. Her hands grasp the fabric of my shirt. She sobs, shoulders shaking against me, and I kiss her hair

I start to rest my chin atop her head, but it stings. I lift it, smoothing her hair down, but my hand comes away stained with blood. Only then do I notice the tiny drop trickling from my busted chin, rolling down my skin.

Rage courses through me, and my hands ache to wrap around Kurt's neck.

But Ari shivers in my arms.

Taking a deep breath, I wrap my arms tighter around her and rest my cheek against her head.

Chapter 10
Kurt

My hands shake on my lap. A single drop of blood trickles down my cheek, and a shiver rolls down my spine in time with its slow progress.

The old couch squeaks as I scoot back. Flies buzz in the kitchen, circling the food left out on the counter. But adrenaline courses through me, and I relish the feel of it.

She deserved it. And so did he.

They deserve so much worse.

My mind fills with choruses of "adulterer" and "philanderer," stirring my rage. It churns within me, and I hate how close I've come to being just like my stupid, weak father.

But no more.

They'll pay for what they did.

I won't stand for it like he always did.

My mind fills with images of the man who showed up to help my mother get her things. I watch my father yell, watch him try to hit my mother as he always did, but the bigger man shoved him back. The man my stupid father couldn't keep her from running to.

Fucking weak.

I watch my father turn on me as soon as she left, picking on the weaker, younger version of me.

But that's not me, now.

My hands curl into fists, and I shake my head. "I'm not weak, anymore."

My pissant of a father paid for what he did to me.

Now, they will, too.

But gravel crunches beneath tires outside, reaching my ears long before the sound of that pitiful engine. My lips curl as I remember the impending return of Kerry and Jake, and for a moment, I panic. My blood runs cold, searching for an answer to give them.

Because they won't understand.

Sheep never understand lions.

They beat a steady path to the door, voices growing closer. Kerry laughs, just like she did when she hit me in the car. The sound grates my nerves. I clench my jaw, grinding my teeth together. My breath speeds up.

The doorknob turns, and the ancient door swings wide, creaking all the way. The pair waft into the house on breezes of their own stupid laughter.

And I sit, statue still, upon the couch. My hands curl tighter, digging my nails into my palms.

They stop in their tracks when they see me. In my periphery, I watch their brows scrunch together, watch them exchange a glance.

Eyes darting to the kitchen doorway, Kerry asks, voice small, "Where are Ariella and Ian?"

"Basement." My jaw barely moves. My teeth barely part. The word comes out a sinister hiss.

"Um…" Kerry stalls.

Putting a reassuring hand on her back, Jake asks, "Why are they down there?"

"Exploring."

"Aw, but we always do that together! Sarah and Tori aren't even here, yet," Kerry exclaims. Disappointment rings clear in her tone, and I shake my head at the stupidity of all this.

Ghosts aren't real, after all. Every stupid trip they've made, every dollar they've spent on their fucking equipment was all a waste.

But my small movement brings my eye out of the shadows, and Jake asks about the mark on my face, the mark that fuckwad, Ian, put there.

But the sheep can't know what awaits them.

"I tripped going down the stupid stairs. Why do you think I came back up?"

"Um, okay…" Kerry drawls. "Do you need anything?"

I stare at her, gaze fierce, and say, "No."

It's a lie. I do need something. I need her and her whipped little dog to leave me alone. I need to show Ariella and Ian why they shouldn't have fucked me over.

But these idiots are in the way.

"Alright, well, I'll put these away," Jake says, lifting a small plastic bag of his wife's brand-new undergarments, volunteering to wait on her, hand and foot. "Would you mind putting the food away, and then, we can go downstairs?"

"Sounds good," she says. "I'm gonna have to ask them why they didn't wait, though. We always explore together. It's just… shitty, you know?"

"I know, sweetheart," Jake says, kissing his wife's forehead. "We'll make sure to give them hell over it, don't worry."

She laughs and moves to the kitchen. Jake disappears into the hall.

And I make my move.

Rising, I mumble something about getting some ice for my face and meander into the kitchen behind Kerry. She turns her back on me easily, underestimating me.

She doesn't even glance back over her shoulder once.

My breath quickens, part rage, part excitement.

Gathering up the remnants of the vegetables, she shoves them into a sack rather unceremoniously and hauls them to the ice chest.

I grab a knife from the cutting board.

Sliding up behind her under the guise of needing ice, I reach around her, clamping one hand over her mouth and plunging the blade into her throat with the other.

A startled gurgle escapes her, but nothing more.

Twisting the blade, I relish the blood gushing out, trickling down the handle of the knife. But it falls short of the violence I crave. My fists ache to drive into her flesh, to crush her face. My veins burn for it.

But she had to be quick.

She had to be quiet.

Lowering her gently to the floor, I jerk the knife free of her flesh and settle it back on the worktable. Blood pours from her neck, and she lifts limp, weak arms to touch the gaping hole. Tears fall over her splattered cheeks, and the pool of blood beneath her envelopes her long hair.

But I'm not done.

And the next one will be so much better.

Chapter 11
Ariella

Pulling back, I wipe tears from my eyes. My hands shake, fingers fluttering against my cheeks. The world threatens to open up and swallow me whole.

But Ian reaches toward me. With a gentle hand beneath my chin, he turns my head to peer at my cheek.

"It's pretty red," he says. He shakes his head and pulls in a deep breath. "You should probably lie down."

My eyes dart to the dingy cot in the corner, the same one Theodore Alton left in here for the people he tortured and killed.

"I think I'll manage…" I answer, not quite brave enough to lie where they suffered. "Besides," I add, looking back at Ian, "you're in worse shape. Let me see your chin."

He tips his head back, wincing as the skin pulls tight.

"I can't tell how bad it is. There's too much blood," I say. But that isn't a good sign. I choke back a sob.

God, this is my fault…

Had I just broken up with Kurt, he wouldn't have been here with us.

And then a terrible thought strikes me.

What would he have done to me if I had broken up with him?

The rage in his eyes as he lashed out at me, his fight with Ian, and the incoherent screaming that followed all flash through my mind, and suddenly I wonder just how deranged he might be.

What kind of monster have I brought down on my friends?

"You know," I say, voice flat and broken. "I almost broke up with Kurt a couple days ago. I wanted to give him one last chance, though. This trip was supposed to help me decide what to do."

A morbid laugh escapes me. "Pretty sure my decision is made, now."

A brittle whimper slips past my lips, and tears cascade over my cheeks. Ian gathers me into his arms.

"It'll be okay," he whispers. "He'll let us out. We just have to wait him out."

My heart twists, and my lungs collapse. Another sob rattles through me as I gaze at the blood dripping from Ian's chin to run down his neck.

"I'm sorry," I mumble. "I shouldn't have brought him here. I'm so sorry."

"Hey, no. Ari, this isn't your fault," Ian gentles, pulling me to him again. "He's an asshole. That isn't your fault."

Strong arms wrap tighter around me, and I lean into Ian's chest, weeping openly.

But footsteps overhead catch our attention.

I freeze, staring at the ceiling.

Is he coming back? Will he let us out? Or is he going to hurt us again?

Chills run down my spine as I imagine the terrible things he could inflict upon us, cornered as we are. But more footsteps creak across the floorboards overhead, sounding out from a different part of the house.

Kerry and Jake.

My veins fill with ice water as I imagine them up there, alone with him. My head fills with all the different things he might be telling them, but none of them quite cover our absence or the food still lying on the table, uncooked.

Will they know something is wrong?

If they do, will he hurt them?

One set of footsteps moves through the house, approaching the bedrooms. Two sets linger in the main rooms, meandering into the kitchen. But only for a moment.

One of them branches off, trailing after the first person, moving toward the bedrooms. My eyes track their progress, moving from one wooden beam to another.

Ian pulls in a deep breath and extricates himself from my embrace. Rising to his feet, he slowly moves toward the door.

But I sit, motionless, on the floor. My heart hammers away at my eardrums, and a sick feeling churns in my belly.

Boards creak, approaching the top of the stairs. I stare in that direction, imagining the dust motes that must swirl beneath those boards. My heart leaps into my throat as I wait.

"Hey, Jake," Ian says, making me jump. "Kerry."

But only silence answers him.

My ragged breathing accelerates, and I curl my hands into fists on my lap.

"Hey!" Jake shouts, still distant, maybe from the top of the stairs.

Then, a solid weight hits the concrete floor beyond our cell, and a sickening snap rings out.

"Fuck! My leg!" Jake shouts. "What the fuck is wrong with you?"

I stare at the cold metal door, listening as Kurt stomps down the stairs. Ian pounds on the door of the cell, screaming at Kurt to stop. Springing to my feet, hating the waves of dizziness that roll through me at the sudden motion, I hammer away at the door.

"Jake, get out of here!" I shout, but the sound of fists meeting flesh fills the basement. "Jake!"

I pound on the door, slamming my fists against it even after the bones threaten to splinter, calling their bluff. "Jake!" I beg, spluttering through tears.

But the struggle beyond the door is short-lived.

Silence descends once more.

Beside me, Ian goes still, hands and head resting on the door. He turns, pressing his ear to the cold metal, straining to hear something, anything.

Barely daring to hope, I whisper, "Jake? Are you okay?" Desperation chokes my words.

No one answers.

"Jake, answer me!"

Time yawns out before us, stretching into an eternity. My frantic heart stumbles in my chest. Ian pulls his ear from the door, rubbing his hands over his face.

When a voice finally speaks beyond the door, my heart stops.

"When will Sarah and Tori get here?" Kurt asks.

But I don't answer his question.

I scream wildly, pounding my hands against the door. "What did you do to him?!"

Fury blazes through me, and I kick the door. Pain shoots through me, but the door does little more than rattle the metal bar in its rack.

"Fine," Kurt says, far too calmly. "I'll wait to deal with you two until after they get here. That way I won't be interrupted."

Ice slithers through me, and I scream at him. "What did you do, Kurt?"

But his feet tread softly up the stairs.

Not caring about my foot, I kick the door again. My poor toes scream in agony. And when I set my foot down, I slip. Ian catches me, but our eyes drop to the floor and the pool of blood seeping under the door.

My stomach drops.

"Ari, stand over there," Ian says.

I scramble away from the door, leaving bloody footprints on cold concrete.

Ian crouches, then lays flat on the floor, careful not to touch the pool of blood or the trail left in my wake.

Peering under the door, he chokes, "Oh my god…"

"No, no, no, no, no…"

He has to be alright. Jake has to be okay.

But that's so much blood…

Unable to wait for Ian to tell me he's alive, just unconscious, I rush forward. Sprawling on the floor, I ignore Ian's protests as he tells me not to look.

But I quickly wish I'd listened.

Jake's hand lies limp, stretched toward the door to our cell. Knuckles busted open and weeping blood, it reaches for us.

But beyond that, the true horror waits.

He stares at us through lifeless eyes. His jaw hangs slack, and a few teeth litter the floor. Blood seeps from his busted lip and caved-in nose, from gashes above his eye.

The shine of too-bright lights on his wedding band catches my eye, easily drawing my gaze from the bloody mess of his face.

And then I realize… only one set of footsteps moves above us.

***

Shock washes over me, drying my tears. I sit there, leaning against the wall in the dank little cell. Ian sits beside me, fingers fidgeting with a loose string ripped from the hem of his t-shirt.

My mind drifts back to my fight with Kurt, and I can't help but wonder where all my confidence went. I've always been so outspoken, so gutsy.

But I've never been tested. Now, facing something truly difficult, facing an actual problem…

I froze.

I failed.

I gulp down a breath, stomach churning uneasily.

And now, because I didn't have the guts to stand up for myself when it mattered, Jake is dead. Kerry probably is, too.

My eyes drift to the ceiling above. I strain my ears, hoping to pick out a second set of footsteps or a whimper, anything to tell me Kerry is still alive. But only Kurt's angry stomps ring out, shaking dust from the ceiling to rain down upon us.

I lean my head back against the wall and close my eyes. Reaching out, I twine my hand with Ian's on his lap, craving the warmth of his touch. I know he doesn't feel the way I do, but…

I need him.

He discards the little string readily, wrapping my hand in both of his. Falling against him, I rest my head on his shoulder and stare out at the little cot across from us.

Silence descends on our cell, punctuated only by the footsteps above. My eyes drift out of focus, half-watching dust motes float through the air. Time oozes past, unmarked, and my mind fills with the sound of Kurt's shouts, the sound of Jake hitting the floor.

"Ari…" Ian begins, pulling me from the sludge filling my mind.

I lift my head, hating the ache that surges through me at the movement. I try not to think about how my face must look.

Ian runs his thumb over the back of my hand, sending little waves of heat through me. His mouth opens, but no words come out. He closes it and looks at me, meeting my gaze for just a second.

A deep breath puffs out his chest, and he shakes his head. "I told myself not to do this. I was just going to stay quiet because you were with Kurt, but now…" He glances at the door of our cell. "Fuck that guy."

A small laugh bursts from me, surprising Ian. His eyes dart to me once more but quickly fall back to our joined hands.

"And… I know this isn't the best timing…" Another deep breath lifts his chest, eyes drifting to the blood drying beneath the door. "But I don't know if I'll get another chance."

His voice cracks.

My heart skips a few beats as my mind grasps at straws, trying to move past the agony beyond the door to figure out what he might say next. Slowly, the world centers on his lips, his thoughts. My entire existence narrows to a single hope, one sweet painful hope.

Finally looking up, Ian meets my desperate gaze. "Ari, I... I'm in love with you."

The breath catches in my lungs, and my heart stops.

His blue eyes fall from mine as he turns my hand over to gaze at my palm. Idly, he traces the lines in it with one finger as he goes on. "I always have been. And when you kissed me back in college... I just froze. I guess I just thought you were too drunk to realize what you were doing."

He shakes his head, letting out a little huff.

"Ian… I knew exactly what I was doing."

He lifts his gaze to meet mine, swallowing.

Seconds trickle past, and I stare at him, wondering if this is real. My heart rattles unsteadily in my chest, shambling along far too quickly. Heat blooms over my skin, coloring my cheeks.

His lips part to speak, drawing my gaze, but the words never come.

And I don't wait for them.

Reaching out, I touch his cheek, careful to avoid the bruising he got while fighting for me. My eyes stray to his lips, and he leans in, inching closer.

After peering into his eyes one last time, my lids fall shut. I brush my lips against his.

And gravity claims us.

Crushing his lips to mine, Ian releases my hand only to slide his fingers into my hair, pulling me to him. My heart expands, threatening to explode, and tears track down my face.

But I cling to Ian, to this kiss that I've waited so long for.

And I hope it won't be our last.

Chapter 12
Ian

Ari slumbers, head cradled on my lap. My head falls back against the wall, lulled by the soft sounds of her breathing. The ebb of adrenaline washes away all my energy as it leaves me.

A sweet, delicate warmth seeps through me as my mind dwells on the feel of Ari's lips on mine. A drowsy smile plays at the corners of my mouth, and for a few moments, I forget the horror of our circumstances.

The scent of Jake's blood lingers in the air. But with my eyes closed to block the sight and the warmth of near-sleep spreading through me, it drifts into the background, like some horrible dream that was just a little too real.

I slip my hand onto Ari's side, relishing the feel of her, the gentle rise and fall of her ribs beneath my palm. Her tears yet stain my jeans, but they're drying fast. Her hair splays over my legs, tickling my skin through a rip in the denim.

A deep breath lifts my chest, flowing out on a contented sigh as Ari shifts, spreading her hand over my thigh.

***

The growl of an engine rumbling up the driveway startles me awake. I jerk my head from the wall, glancing nervously around and hoping for half a breath that it was all just a terrible dream, that Jake and Kerry are fine, that Kurt didn't hit Ari.

But the cement cell holds us, just as it did before my eyes closed. My body aches from sitting on cold concrete. I can only imagine how Ari must feel, having slept on it.

Outside, the car revs to draw our attention, and I know Tori must be driving. The massive V-8 growls, but her love for the car and its power doesn't pull a smile to my lips like it normally would. Dread seeps into my stomach, oozing and churning violently.

Because if we heard her, Kurt must have.

And I don't dare hope he's seen the error in his ways.

Glancing at the door, I hold back my gorge as my gaze rakes over the blood that crept into the cell. It glares at me, berating me for not doing better, for not knocking the shit out of Kurt when I had the chance.

For staying away from Ari for the past few months when she needed someone to talk to.

Maybe I could have swayed her. Maybe I could have helped her see something was wrong with this sick fuck.

But I was too busy being a damn coward.

Gritting my teeth, I resolve to do better, to *be* better. Being a coward won't help me, now.

"Ari," I whisper.

A gentle shake of her shoulder rouses her, and she pushes herself bolt upright. Her entire body goes rigid as she takes in the cell we still sit in. Fear laces her eyes when she turns to look at me.

"It was real…" she mumbles, shaking her head. Her eyes fall from mine, fluttering as they slip to the concrete beneath her hands.

My heart breaks to see her like this, and I can only nod.

It's real.

But we don't have time to dwell on it, right now.

"Tori and Sarah just pulled in," I say, tone deliberately quiet. Kurt's footsteps ring out above us, but I can't stomach the idea of drawing him down here with Ari, again.

Her eyes dart to the ceiling, staring intently in the direction of the driveway as if her gaze could pierce through the house to show her the scene outside by sheer force of will.

My heart freezes as Kurt stomps toward the front door. He pauses there, waiting, and I strain my ears.

Tori shuts her car off, doubtless confused as to why we haven't all rushed out to greet them. My pulse pounds unevenly, and my breath comes quickly. But I don't hear footsteps on gravel. I don't hear laughter or voices outside. Too much concrete and earth lay between us and them for me to gauge their progress toward the door.

I count the seconds.

We have to warn them…

They have no idea what kind of mad man awaits them, just inside the door.

The floorboards creak as Kurt shifts his weight. A few dust motes flutter through the air, catching the light.

I swallow.

Rising to my feet, I position myself just below where Kurt stands. Ari comes to join me, placing a tentative hand on the small of my back. Our eyes never drop from the wooden beams supporting Kurt's weight.

An insane frenzy threatens to grip me, to send my fists flying at those boards, hoping to cave them in beneath him. But I hold myself steady, gritting my teeth.

Seconds creep by as we listen. My heart hammers away in my chest, dreading what I fear might happen if Sarah or Tori opens the door.

And then, I hear it.

A single laugh punctuates the air as they approach the front porch. Footsteps creak on the old boards, protesting even their light frames and the small duffel bags they always bring on these trips.

We have to warn them.

So, I do the only thing I can, locked in this stupid cell. I shout at the top of my lungs, begging them to hear me, willing my voice to carry through the floor and the cement and the porch.

Ari follows my lead, screaming bloody murder.

And their approach halts on the front porch. No more footsteps assail our ears, carrying our friends into the hands of a maniac. One more board creaks, and my heart stops.

Please… Just turn away. Go get help, something.

Just don't come in here.

My throat rasps, but I keep screaming, keep yelling for them to run as fast and as far as they can. Beside me, Ari's voice breaks with the intensity of her fury and fear, crackling out before she renews her efforts to save our friends.

Overhead, a board creaks as Kurt shifts his weight, once more.

Chapter 13
Kurt

A cacophony erupts beneath me as Ian and Ariella start screaming. I grind my teeth together, hating them more intensely with every breath. My fingers tighten around the handle of the cast iron skillet until my knuckles go white.

They'll pay for this later.

My quarry stills on the porch outside, just a few feet shy of opening the door. Fury roils within me, and my muscles ache to release the tension. But outside, the girls freeze. The boards groan as one of them drops a bag.

"What was that…?" a soft voice whispers beyond the door.

Which bitch was that?

I comb through my memory, trying to put a name with a voice, but only halfheartedly. It doesn't matter. They're in my way. They both have to go.

Stepping gingerly across the porch, one of them approaches the window, and I shrink back against the wall. I flatten myself against it, unwilling to relinquish the element of surprise, even if Ariella and that fuck, Ian, already partially ruined it.

Maybe the idiots will think it's one of those ghosts they always try so hard to catch.

I scoff under my breath, wondering how I ever got mixed up in all their crap. Stupid Ariella. So naïve, so much of an idiot to think ghosts real, to think herself capable of getting evidence when so many others have failed before her.

The arrogance of it makes my blood boil, yet it pales next to the arrogance of bringing me along just so she could fuck Ian in the next room.

My grip tightens on the skillet now hanging beside me. I settle it gently against the wall so it doesn't bang against it.

"I'm going to call them," the other girl says on the porch. "Something seems… off."

"Oh, you mean the screams?" the first girl says. "Yeah, I'd say that's a little off."

"You know what I mean," the second one, maybe Sarah, adds, defensive and hurt.

Weak little bitch.

"Sorry," Tori says. "I'm just worried."

"No service," Sarah complains. "Do you think they're hurt?"

"I don't…" But Tori's words cut off.

I glance toward the window, see her peering through with hands cupped against the glass to block the light from outside. And for a split second, realization dawns across her features.

"Sarah…" she whispers, and I know she's seen me. "Sarah, come on."

Goosebumps prick my skin, raising the hairs on my arms. They beat a frantic pace across the porch, old wood complaining noisily beneath them.

And I rip the door open, giving chase.

Tori half drags Sarah as they flee, and the shorter girl's long blonde locks flutter in the wind. They sprint across the lawn, leaving the continued shouts of Ian and Ariella behind in favor of their own. All around me, screams fill the air, and I drink it in. Power courses through me, warming my blood and pushing me out the door.

But the straps of their goddamn bag wrap around my foot, sending me headlong down the stairs. I do all I can to roll, to absorb the force of the landing, but the skillet catches a stair, bending one finger at an odd angle with a pop and a sharp lance of pain.

But I'm on my feet in an instant, running after them.

They can't get away...

The setting sun casts long shadows over them, intensifying the fear in their eyes when they look back at me. And my heart pumps just a little harder, beats just a little faster.

They're afraid of me.

As they should be.

My feet pound the earth into submission, propelling me closer and closer to them.

Tori, the taller one with the sides of her head shaved, reaches the driver's door, pushing Sarah to the back of the car before jerking her own door open. The little blonde doesn't even bother going to the other side, climbing into the back seat of the big black car, certainly more to my taste than Ian's car.

The engine bursts to life as I reach the sedan. I stare in at their shocked faces, relishing the horror in their eyes as they stare out at me.

And I bash the skillet against the window.

It splinters, sending shards of safety glass in every direction. A chorus of shrieks erupts from within the car, and I smile. Jerking the skillet free, I pull back to slam it into the side of Tori's face.

But she stomps the gas, rocketing backward and turning as she goes.

The stupid bitch nearly runs my toes over in the process.

Sprinting after her, I catch her as she hits Ian's pitiful little car. My lips curl upward at the crunch of the puny thing giving way.

Serves him right. Even the lesbian knows better than to drive such a shitty little thing.

Hauling my arm back, I bring the skillet up for another swing, then drive it down toward Sarah. She screams as it connects, spraying her with little pellets of glass.

But her scream dies on her lips when the skillet plunges just a little further, smashing against her forehead. She sprawls over the seat just as Tori punches the gas again, kicking up gravel and dust as she speeds away from me.

Fury guides my arm, and I launch the skillet at the car. It bashes into the rear windshield, splintering it and getting stuck in the safety glass.

And rage simmers in my gut.

For a long time, I stare after them, listening to the roar of the engine as they drive away.

But I know I won't have much time, now.

Fury fills me, curling my fingers into claws. The world narrows to contain nothing more than my galloping heart and my labored breathing.

Turning to face the house, I grit my teeth and focus on how good it'll feel to spill the traitors' blood.

Chapter 14
Ariella

Fear trickles down my spine, riding on cold beads of sweat. My eyes fall shut as I strain my ears to pick out what's happening outside. The hairs on the back of my neck stand on end, but eventually, Tori's car speeds away.

They're safe…

I breathe a sigh of relief, but it's short-lived.

With them gone, Kurt will surely come for us. I don't dare hope Tori hit him with her car, spilling his blood across the driveway.

Please get the cops here soon.

Despite leaving religion behind in my childhood, I whisper a prayer, begging for help. Because whatever snapped in Kurt made him far more dangerous than I ever thought he could be.

And I don't know if we can take him.

He held his own far too well in his fight with Ian. He already killed Jake…

My throat tightens, and I choke back a sob.

He beat him to death, like some barbarian. He probably killed Kerry. He is not the man I thought he was.

And I didn't even think highly of him.

The full breadth of how wrong I was about him settles on my shoulders, weighing me down with the lives of my friends. My heart stutters in my chest, sucking my ribs inward.

My eyes snap open as my knees buckle, but I steady myself with a hand on the wall. Ian reaches out, grabbing my waist to help keep me upright.

Had I just broken it off with him before this trip, had I seen him for what he was…

Looking back, the red flags burn bright in my mind. All the things that made me mad, all the things I decided to ignore for the sake of giving him one more chance…

All the things I should have recognized for what they were now scream at me in Jake's voice, Kerry's voice.

And it's my fault…

I lost them because I looked the other way.

But I'll be damned if I lose anyone else to this psycho.

I pull in a shaky breath, nodding as resolution fills me.

Turning around, stepping slowly on wobbly legs, I face Ian. "Will you help me take this cot apart?"

***

Dust floats into the air as Kurt stomps through the house above us. He screams incoherently for a while, and thuds sound out as heavy objects crash down. Ian snaps another board in the little cot, tearing apart history in a way that makes my insides ache.

But something tells me the tortured ghosts in this place would appreciate it, eager to aid our escape attempt in any way possible. Glancing around at the cell, I wonder what they think of their home, the site of their torment, their murders, being turned into a museum of sorts.

What must they think of this recent turn of events, this repetition of history?

Fabric tears, sending a shiver down my spine as Ian shreds the cot. He hands me a board with long rusty nails sticking out of the end, and I test its weight.

Nodding, I try to convince myself that this will work.

Insanity threatens to grip me, to throw me over the edge into a chasm of panic. My eyes unfocus, fixed on the board in my hand without actually seeing it.

This is my life, now.

Fighting to live…

Killing to live?

I swallow hard.

Is this what it's come to? Can I do it? Can I kill him?

Ian puts a tender hand on my cheek, drawing my attention. My eyes fix on him, tracing the lines of his face and plumbing the depths of those blue eyes. The marks of Kurt's fists mar his features. I nod.

I can do it.

If it comes down to killing Kurt or losing Ian… I can do it.

I grit my teeth, praying that I don't lose my nerve, that I don't freeze. Flashes of the confrontation earlier flicker through my mind, but Ian wasn't in harm's way, then. Only me.

And I had no idea the monster that stood before me.

Now, I know.

I pull in a deep breath, and we move toward the door. Careful not to step in the puddle of drying blood, *Jake's blood*, we stand on either side of the door, waiting.

Because we know he's coming for us.

We just don't know when.

Seconds spread out before me, stretching to feel like years. Time slows to an agonizing crawl as Kurt destroys the home above us.

One final crash shakes the house, then silence rings loud, pressing down on me. I glance at Ian, heart hammering in my chest. I swallow hard, trying to keep my hands from shaking.

He offers up a reassuring smile and tightens his hold on his own board. Softly, he whispers, "I'm here. I won't let him hurt you again."

My insides lurch, caught somewhere between the intense relief of knowing I can finally be with Ian and the soul-shattering fear of losing him. But determination steels my resolve.

I can't lose him.

I won't let that happen.

I pull in a deep breath. Shuffling my board from one hand to the other, I wipe my sweaty palms on my pants. Doubt lingers in the back of my mind, whispering cruelly that we'll die, that Kurt will overpower us easily.

We just have to make it until Sarah and Tori get help.

They'll get help.

Maybe they'll get someone out here before Kurt even comes downstairs.

But footsteps break the silence upstairs.

And I know I was a fool to hope.

Chapter 15
Ian

My heart pounds against my ribs. The roar of my blood rushing through my veins nearly drowns out the sound of Kurt's footsteps on the stairs, but I strain my ears, desperate not to lose track of him.

Ari's board trembles in the air, held in a white-knuckled grip. Swallowing, I try to steady my nerve, to prepare for the mongrel that lurks beyond the door.

After all, he's flesh and blood. He can be killed.

I just don't know if I can do it.

Swallowing back the lump in my throat, I glance at Ari one more time, rethinking the plan to stand on opposite sides of the door. I need to stand between her and him. I need to protect her.

I can't let him hurt her again.

My lungs falter at the idea of him getting his hands on her.

But the thought is cut short.

"Time to pay…" Kurt sneers as he approaches the door. "The bitch and the boy-toy… But you didn't know who you were dealing with, who you were *fucking over*."

My blood runs cold. Every fiber of my being aches to defend Ari against this asshole's accusations, but I grit my teeth to keep from shouting at him. We need to surprise him.

"Now, I'm sure you're expecting me to come in there to drag you out, Ariella. You've never been the brightest," he says, and my stomach turns. "But let's make one thing clear. That isn't happening. You're going to walk out, by yourself, and then you're going to close the door on your little Casanova. Then, you're going with me to the barn."

Like hell…

Rage slithers through me, coiling in my belly. A glance at Ari finds her similarly affected, face contorted into a scowl.

"Want to know why you're going to turn yourself in for punishment?" Kurt asks, and the words chill me to my core. Dread weighs on me as he steps up to the door. "Have you wondered where that bitch, Kerry, is?"

Ice water flows through me.

"She's upstairs, though she hasn't heard much of this. She's out cold, tied up. There's a lot I *could* do to her…" Kurt says, voice lingering sickeningly. "But if you come with me, Ariella, if you go willingly… She won't suffer quite so much."

Metal slides on metal, grating as Kurt slips the bar free of our cell door. I tighten my hold on the board in my hands, tensing every muscle in my body as I wait. The metal bar clatters to the floor, and the door creaks open.

I shoot Ari a look, shaking my head. "Don't go," I mouth. "Stay put." I gesture at the floor beneath her feet emphatically, trying to make her see that she can't go out there.

After all, Kurt isn't exactly stable. We can't trust him.

Luring him through that door is our only chance.

But tears track down Ari's cheeks. Her brows furrow, and her lips quiver. She shakes her head.

I know a losing battle when I see one.

I'm going to lose her…

My insides clench painfully. "Please, Ari," I beg, shaking my head. "Stay here."

"I can't," she whispers. "I can't let him hurt her."

She steps forward into Jake's dried blood, turning to face the open door, and my heart lurches. Panic trickles in, threatening to overwhelm me.

"Be a good girl and drop that, won't you?" Kurt says.

Ari's board falls to the floor at her feet. "You have to swear you won't hurt

Kerry," she says, bargaining with a psycho. She lifts her hands into the air.

But I can't let this happen.

Rushing forward, I duck under her arms, squeezing between her and the doorframe. With all the force I can muster, I slam into Kurt. We fly through the air, crashing down hard on the cement floor.

I land solidly on Kurt's chest, and all the air whooshes out of him, rank breath breaking on my face. He brings something solid down on my back, and pain rockets through me. I haul my fist back, landing a solid hit to his nose. It breaks, and blood gushes over his face.

But some strange mania pulls him into a fit of laughter, speckling my face with his blood.

He slams something heavy down on my back again, and the sharp snap of a broken rib tears through me. A scream rips its way free of my throat, and Kurt flips me over.

Straddling me, he lifts a cast iron pot over his head, ready to bring it down onto my face.

My life flashes before my eyes in little bits and pieces. My mother's funeral and the grief that followed. Fractured images of Ari laughing, the smile on my father's face at my college graduation, the smile I shattered when I told him I was going to culinary school after that.

I didn't even message him back earlier…

And now, I'll never get the chance.

Chapter 16
Ariella

Kurt and Ian tangle on the floor, and shock holds me still for a heartbeat. Ian's fist slams into Kurt's nose, and blood pours out.

But laughter fills the air, speckling Ian's face with droplets of crimson.

The pure, unadulterated sound of insanity shakes me loose, and I stoop, grabbing the board I dropped just seconds ago.

My battered heart stutters in my chest as Kurt slams a solid iron pot into Ian's back, pulling an anguished scream from his lungs. My stomach plummets as Kurt rolls Ian over, and raises the pot over his head.

I swing, throwing all my weight behind the board and its rusted nails. The board connects with Kurt's shoulder, nails sinking into flesh. Kurt screams as he topples over, ripping the board from my hands. Splinters dig into my palms.

Kurt lays sprawled over Jake's battered body, whimpering in pain. Blood gushes out beneath the board. He yanks it free with a squelching sound, gasping as the nails leave his flesh.

But I'm already moving, pulling Ian to his feet.

He groans, placing a hand on his ribs.

But we have to move.

We have to get out of here.

Sprinting up the stairs, I grit my teeth against Ian's moans of pain. His arm drapes over my shoulder, leaning on me more heavily than I'd like. Not because I don't want to help him.

But because I'm not sure how far I can help him along like this.

Every step, every jarring leap up the stairs, must send jolts of pain through his ribs, but we can't stop.

Can he drive like this?

Suddenly, I'm glad he taught me to drive stick. Memories of those sunny afternoons in his car warm my heart, but I don't get time to enjoy them.

As we crest the top of the stairs, Kurt shouts, "Ariella, you fucking bitch! You stupid whore!"

I push myself faster, feet pounding the floor as Ian and I run through the hall. Behind me, I hear a board slam into the cement floor hard enough to splinter. My heart pounds in my ears, almost loud enough to drown out the scrape of an iron pot on concrete. Ian's ragged breathing in my ear does its best to shield me from the sound of Kurt slipping in Jake's blood and falling back to the floor with an outraged howl.

Careening around the corner, I nearly go down. Blood pools on the kitchen floor, reaching out into the rest of the house. Kerry lays broken by the icebox, throat cut wide open and grinning at me like a grotesque second mouth.

I barely catch my balance, barely hold back the bile creeping up my throat.

Her hair sprawls out in her blood, clumping together as the crimson liquid dries. Her once-beautiful eyes stare at me, empty and cold. My feet stumble, slowing me. A knife rests on the work table, shining red in the dim light. I grab it, mesmerized by the morbid object.

And Ian pushes me along, picking up the slack as I falter.

We rush into the living room, and a wall steals her corpse from my view. Broken porcelain plates crunch underfoot as we dodge broken couches and toppled curio cabinets, making our way to the door.

Just as Kurt shouts at us from the top of the stairs.

My hand tightens on the knife handle as we burst through the door. The darkness of a moonless night coats the world. A single spear of light reaches out from the door behind us, punctuating the inky black of a night in the forest.

Sprinting, we descend the stairs, vaulting over Tori's discarded duffel bag.

"Fuck," Ian groans as he lands, holding a hand to his ribs.

His little blue car sits in the driveway, waiting for us on the other side of a copse of trees. Barely visible, it taunts us with the promise of safety.

Stumbling through the underbrush, we try to take the most direct route. But Kurt launches himself out of the house after us.

A solid weight slams into Ian's leg with a hollow, metallic clang, dropping him to the ground. His arm around my shoulder pulls me down beside him, and the knife slips from my grasp, sliding into brambles.

And then, Kurt finds us.

A kick to the gut curls me in on myself, transforming me into a whimpering ball of agony. Pain spirals through me, sapping my strength.

For a moment, the world tumbles into complete darkness as I close my eyes. Coming up onto hands and knees, I coat the ground with the remnants of my lunch. Each move, every wrenching heave sends shockwaves of pain through me.

But my hand finds the familiar handle of the knife. My fingers curl around it, grateful to have it back.

I look up, hoping to have an easy target.

Beside me, thrashing in the brush, Ian kicks and fights to keep Kurt at bay. But he's found the cast iron pot, and he raises it high. Ian jerks to the side, flinching, moving his head just in time to avoid most of the hit.

But not enough. He goes slack beneath Kurt.

Launching myself at Kurt, I knock him off of Ian. His greasy black hair sprawls on the ground beneath him, shadows reaching out into the dark of the night.

My heart beats frantically as I drive the knife down into Kurt's chest, once, twice. It takes everything I have, every bit of strength. His blood pours out, splattering and spraying over me as I pull the knife free, only to slam it home again.

Gasping, he clutches at his chest, but I drive the blade down again, severing one of his fingers in the process. I pull the knife free, then bring it down into the soft flesh of his neck.

The life fades from Kurt's eyes. He goes still beneath me, and I fall to the ground beside him, shaking.

But I don't bother to catch my breath.

Crawling to Ian's side, I take his face in my hands. His eyes flutter, and tears prick at the corners of my eyes.

He's alive!

Relief washes through me, and I kiss him, tender yet fierce.

"Ari," he mumbles against my lips.

"Shh…" I whisper. "It's okay, now. We just need to get you to the hospital."

"Are we… safe?" Ian asks.

I choke back a sob as exhaustion washes over me. "We're safe," I assure him.

Pushing myself to my feet, I brace myself against a tree as fresh waves of agony burst through me. My stomach aches, and my ribs protest every movement.

Leaning, I reach out a hand for Ian, hoping he can stand. Then, I notice the gash on his forehead where the cast iron pot glanced off his skull. Blood drips at a steady pace, leaving him behind as it leaps to the ground.

His eyes flutter, staying closed for far too long before they drift open again.

I'll have to drag him to the car…

Desperation wells within me at the prospect.

Am I strong enough?

Crouching beside his head, I loop my arms under his. Pain bursts through me as I try to tug him along, and lights flash across my vision. Falling to the ground with an anguished cry, I snap.

Tears pour from my eyes, and I scream into the night, shouting at the world for all it's put me through tonight.

"Over here!" a strange, deep voice calls, moving closer and closer to me.

And then I realize the flashing lights aren't in my mind.

Red and blue lights play across the trees around me. The beam of a flashlight lands upon my face. I instinctively jerk my arm up to shield my eyes and gasp with the pain that shudders through me at the movement.

It's one thing too many, and I fall backward, slumping into the brush. My eyes close as the world spins around me.

And darkness closes in.

Epilogue
Ariella

Laying my head down on Ian's hospital bed, I stare at our entwined fingers. The machines monitoring his vitals beep steadily, reassuring me that he's alive.

If only he'd wake up…

The doctors begged me for patience, urged me to stay in bed, promising that he'd come around soon.

It's only been a few hours…

But that's a few hours too long.

My heart lurches, and tears prick at the corners of my eyes.

"Come back to me…" I whisper.

A knock sounds at the door, and I jerk upright, instantly regretting the sudden motion. My broken ribs scream at me, and I nearly double over.

"Sorry," Tori says, brows reaching for each other.

"I thought you heard us coming," Sarah adds from her wheelchair.

Tori pushes her further into the room, and Sarah tugs her IV pole along. Her blonde hair lays in delicate waves on her shoulders, freshly cleaned of the blood that leaked from her forehead earlier. A patch of gauze glows in the fluorescent lighting, covering the stitches.

I shake my head, careful to keep the motion contained to my head and neck. "I didn't hear you."

"I didn't, either," Ian whispers.

I jerk my head toward him, and suddenly, I don't care about my ribs. Springing to my feet, gritting my teeth against the pain that reaches through every synapse, I kiss him. Desperate to feel the life pulsing through him, to know that he's with me, I put a hand to the side of his neck.

His heart beats steadily beneath my fingers, and the monitor beside us beeps a little faster.

"I was so afraid you wouldn't come back," I whisper, lips brushing over his.

Hand tangling in my hair, he smiles up at me. "Of course, I came back. I don't want to be a ghost just yet. I want to be with you, first."

We laugh, both grimacing at the pain that courses through us.

Slowly, I ease myself back down into my chair. But my eyes never leave his. I wrap both my hands around his, twining our fingers.

A few errant tears trickle over my cheeks, but I don't bother to wipe them away.

Clearing my throat, I say, "Your dad's on his way, maybe about another hour? I called him as soon as I could."

"Thank you." Ian pulls in a deep breath, clenching his jaw against the pain. "I have a lot to tell him. That'll give me time to figure out how."

About the Author

Elexis Bell is a quiet nerd with too many hobbies, including everything from gaming to shower-singing and even archery, weather permitting. She specializes in sarcasm and writing stories that make people feel. She's made a home for herself with her husband and a small army of cats.

She writes dark, gritty stories, sprinkling gut-wrenching emotions over high fantasy romance, thrillers, post-apocalyptic romance, and science fiction.

For further information, follow her on Instagram, Twitter, or Facebook, or check out her blog on her website. There, you can sign up for her newsletter to stay up to date on all future book releases, giveaways, and on-going projects.

www.elexisbell.com

Other Books by this Author
All available here:
http://author.to/ElexisBell

Annabelle

Vigilante justice thriller set in a western? Weaponized parasol? Yes, please.

Allmother Rising

Gods and grudges, magic and animal companions? Straight and LGBT romance? Yes, please.

Soul Bearer

The return of dragons? Slow burn romance? A part-Orc, underdog of a heroine? Yes, please.

World for the Broken

Slow burn romance in a dark, post-apocalyptic world? No holds barred, no punches pulled? Yes, please.

A Heart of Salt & Silver

Blood and broken hearts? Immortals, magic, and inner demons? Yes, please.

The Gem of Meruna

Oppression and a magical gem that can defeat a dictator? Slow burn romance? Yes, please.